This Little Tiger book belongs to:

This book is for Nicholas and Norinda
~ A M

For my godson Liam
~ A E

LITTLE TIGER PRESS
1 The Coda Centre, 189 Munster Road, London SW6 6AW
www.littletiger.co.uk

First published in Great Britain 2010
This edition published 2011

Text copyright © Angela McAllister 2010
Illustrations copyright © Alison Edgson 2010
Angela McAllister and Alison Edgson have asserted their rights
to be identified as the author and illustrator of this work under
the Copyright, Designs and Patents Act, 1988

A CIP catalogue record for this book is available from the British Library

LTP/1900/0883/0314 · Printed in China

4 6 8 10 9 7 5

YUCK!
That's not a Monster!

Angela McAllister · Alison Edgson

LITTLE TIGER PRESS
London

Mr and Mrs Monster were very
proud of their three eggs.
Mr Monster kept them warm by
huffing with his hot, stinky breath.
Mrs Monster screeched to them.

One stormy night,
the first egg cracked.
Out climbed an ugly
little monster, with
prickly spikes and
snarly fangs.
"Aaah! He's FRIGHTFUL!"
sighed Mr and Mrs
Monster happily. So that's
what they called him.

Then the second egg cracked.
Out climbed another
ugly little monster,
with horny spines and
bristly warts.
"Oooh! She's HORRID!"
gasped Mr and Mrs Monster
happily. So that's what
they called her.

Then the third egg shook a bit. Frightful
and Horrid gave it a poke. Out crept
something very soft and pink.
"UGH! HE'S SWEET!!"
said the little monsters.
"LET'S SQUASH HIM!"

"Well, he's not what we expected," said Mrs Monster. "He is a bit of a shock."

"Let's throw him in the rubbish bin," said Mr Monster.

Suddenly there was a crash of thunder.

"*Mama!*" cried the fluffy one and jumped into Mrs Monster's arms. She looked down at her bundle of sweetness. "I think we'll keep him," she said. "He may look different but inside he is a monster, just like us."

So they called him Little Shock.

Each day Frightful and Horrid
grew hairier and scarier.

They learnt how to spit and
hiss and snarl and scratch.

But Little Shock grew MORE
fluffy. He liked to gurgle and roly-poly
and twinkle his big blue eyes. He loved
his brother and sister and followed
them everywhere.

"If you want to play with us you've got to be wild and rampageous," said Frightful and Horrid.

They showed him how to howl at the moon until it hid behind a cloud. But Little Shock was afraid of the dark.

They showed him how to squash and stamp
and trample. But Little Shock saw a worried
worm and sat down to give it a hug.
"Ugh!" sneered Frightful and Horrid.
"He's just a cutie-pie!"

Soon Frightful and Horrid were bold enough
to go monstering in the wood.

"You must take your brother with you," insisted
Mrs Monster.

Frightful and Horrid snorted grumpily but
they put Little Shock in a trolley, hid him under
a blanket and tugged him along.

In the wood, Frightful leapt out at a fox and made its fur turn white. Horrid pounced on a wild pig and made it jump into a tree. They had a wonderful time!

GRRR!

Little Shock cuddled his blanket
and played peek-a-boo with a mouse.

"What shall we do now?"
said Frightful.
"Let's find something big
to scare," said Horrid.
Something big rustled in the
bushes ahead, so they crept up on it.
Frightful and Horrid saw a hairy hump.
They winked at each other, took
a deep breath and . . .

But the hairy hump was only a little bit of a BIG monster! It snarled and flashed its fiery eyes. "WHO DARED TO ROAR AT ME?"

Frightful and Horrid were
too terrified to run away.
Their spines shrivelled and
their claws curled up.

Suddenly the BIG monster
spotted Little Shock.
    "OOOH! CANDYFLOSS!"
he said.
    Little Shock stared up at the
monster's face. His big blue eyes
grew wider and wider . . .

Then **MWAH!**
He gave the monster
a kiss right on
the cheek!

"YEUCH!"

The BIG monster wailed and dropped Little Shock in horror. He was so afraid that his fur turned to frizz and his bristles fell out.

"HELP!" he cried. "IT'S
ADORABLE!"
    And he ran away, crying
for his mummy.

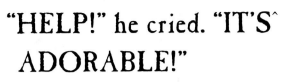

Frightful and Horrid couldn't
believe their eyes.
    "You kissed him! You
kissed him!" they laughed.

Horrid swung her little brother high in the air
and sat him on Frightful's shoulders.

"Maybe being cute could be useful after all,"
she said, giving him a pinch.

Little Shock just purred happily.

"Come on, then," said Frightful proudly,
"let's go home and ALL kiss Mum and Dad!"

More MONSTROUS reads
from Little Tiger Press!

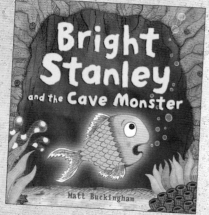

Bright Stanley and the Cave Monster

Matt Buckingham

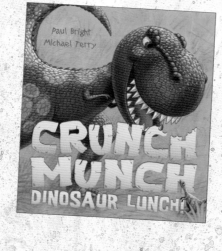

Paul Bright
Michael Terry

CRUNCH MUNCH DINOSAUR LUNCH!

There's No Such Thing As MONSTERS!

Steve Smallman   Caroline Pedler

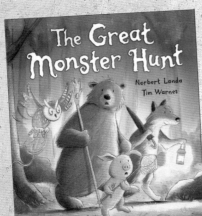

The Great Monster Hunt

Norbert Landa
Tim Warnes

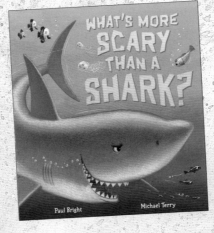

WHAT'S MORE SCARY THAN A SHARK?

Paul Bright   Michael Terry

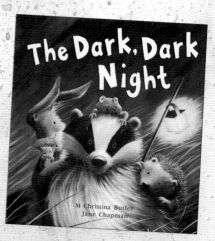

The Dark, Dark Night

M Christina Butler
Jane Chapman

For information regarding any of the above titles
or for our catalogue, please contact us:
Little Tiger Press, 1 The Coda Centre,
189 Munster Road, London SW6 6AW
Tel: 020 7385 6333 • Fax: 020 7385 7333
E-mail: contact@littletiger.co.uk • www.littletiger.co.uk